# Peregrine

2018　Volume XXXII

| | |
|---:|:---|
| **Managing Editors** | ELLEN SUMMERS |
| | JANET SUMMERS |
| **Poetry Editors** | RACHELLE M. PARKER |
| | ELLEN SUMMERS |
| **Prose Editor** | JANET SUMMERS |
| **Emerging Voices Editor** | KAREN BUCHINSKY |
| **Layout** | LANE GODDARD |
| **Publisher** | PAT SCHNEIDER |

Amherst Writers & Artists Press, Inc.
P.O. Box 1076
Amherst, MA 01004
Phone: 413 253 3307

peregrine@amherstwriters.org
www.amherstwriters.org

*Peregrine* is published annually. Submission details are available at amherstwriters.org or peregrinejournal.submittable.com. Payment is in copies. The editors endorse the practice of simultaneous submissions.

Copies are available on Amazon.com for $12.

Amherst Writers & Artists (AWA) affiliates offer writing workshops for adults, youth, and children across the world. In addition, AWA sponsors public readings and maintains an international training program that supports the work of writers and artists. Amherst Writers & Artists Press, Inc., publishes *Peregrine*, books of poetry and fiction, and the Amherst Writers & Artists poetry chapbook series.

*Cover art by Barry Moser (used with permission)*
*Peregrine nesting sketch by Karen Buchinsky (used with permission)*

## Contributors

# BERNADETTE D. McCOMISH

## Slipstream

The sand in my sheet is evidence
of the beached whale you were in another life. At night
I heard you sing humpback in your sleep as I
tried to crush myself under your fins.
Because my larynx was unable
to produce baleen sounds
you'd understand, I kissed
with my eyelashes, thumbed the backs of your knees
with bubblegum oil until your land snore returned.
Frequency was vital; the signs
on the seabed said DEAD END in yellow
metal diamonds, and all we had
was your song, my lips, and an echo
to channel us home.

## At 4 a.m. on a Sunday Morning

I do not want to lose you.
Yet burgundy fluid flows from your body
Almost the color of our favorite wine,
And I watch it, wipe it away, dab the sheets with cold cold water

So the drops won't leave a trail
To remind me
You are fallible.
You are human.

You might slip away from me without much warning, without me having a
chance to prepare.
Stop.
Stop. Stop. Stop.
We are not there, We are not There. We are Not there, yet.

We are in the trough of the wave, waiting
For the test results to tell us
If it's sooner or later.
I prefer later, much much later. Days, weeks, months, years later until we have

Flown to Africa to see her people, her sky, her animals,
Snorkeled with coral and teal fish in the Galapagos,
Returned to the Cape where we will bike to Wellfleet,
And ravish each other after a cold beer and oysters.
It is Monday. Tomorrow is Tuesday. We will know Wednesday.

Hold on. I'm a lifeguard. Hold on to me as I swim us through,
Steady I stand despite these undercurrents,
I step my way over the sharp rocks with my rubber water shoes
And we will ride my Rescue Surf Board
Into the shore.

I am ready. I've done this.
I've got you covered, with salty tears, weary arms, and my hope
That will sustain us until the next storm.

## Day of Lights

I didn't understand at the tender age of six why the floating lanterns we released every year on Day of Lights were scarlet. I was just caught up in the beauty every year, the warm ambiance the lights released, glowing in the dark sky. I saw them as a light to the heavens, that maybe if I didn't let go to release the lights they would carry me up to the skies where I would say hello to Haraja, Mother of the Gods and Goddess of the Harvest. I would ask her to make my village's year prosperous and in return she would give me a gift, for being so unselfish with my one request to her. But I would see through her clever trick and ask for nothing so as to not let the sin of greed sweep me away. Then we would talk and laugh together and have lots of fun.

The next year my father was dead.

Papi was a warm presence throughout my childhood. He was always away traveling for his business, but it seemed whenever I was hurt or needed him, he would come and sweep me off my feet, spinning me around and telling me stories. I used to think he was a magical genie who came when I called, but also had other important deeds to carry out. I always wanted him to stay when he had to leave, so I would cry for days. The last time he left Mami was crying, so I clutched his leg and begged him not to leave. Later in the day when I asked Mami where he went, she was silent for a very long time before telling me in a whispery voice, worn out from sobbing, that he was protecting us. When I said I thought he could do that better at home, she turned away from me and told me not to ask her the question again.

When I was seven, on the Day of Lights, a man from the government came to our door. I remember that our house then was newer than the rest of the houses in the village. It was a bright white, and the floor was a wood flooring, different than some of my friends, who had dirt or tile flooring.

I was so proud of that floor until the man came in. His nice leather shoes seemed like they were too nice for our scuffed floor, and I hung my head in shame. His eyes were shifty and sad as he handed a piece of paper to Mami. She read it slowly and then started to scream. She was sobbing, shaking his shoulders and asking questions that I could barely make out. The government man was clearly disturbed and unused to such a violent outburst. I tried to distance myself from Mami, shamed by my mother's actions. He was about to leave when he saw me standing in the corner. Still fending off my mother's attack, he looked at me and mumbled, "May the wind dry your tears," a traditional comforting expression for the loss of a loved one. It was only then that I realized someone had died.

I assumed that it was maybe Auntie Chadra. She had a bad heart and Papi worked hard so he could help her buy her heart medicine. Or perhaps it was Uncle Vadrin. He, too, had health problems, and as the eldest brother he was growing frail. It was only when my mother wailed my father's name that I understood. He was dead. He had died protecting us. And he was never, ever coming back to swing me around the courtyard.

The days passed in a grey blur. The only thing that made me excited, the only thing that I focused on now was the Day of Lights. I thought maybe if I clutched the lantern hard enough I would float up to the heavens and be reunited with Papi.

Normally we put a candle in our lanterns, nothing more. It's strong enough to lift them but not enough to carry someone away. I knew that I would need something better to lift me off to Papi, so I stole a candle from the temple. They were more powerful than our government-rationed household candles because they needed to stay lit for days on a time. I felt bad, but then rationalized the choice by reminding myself that I would see all the gods soon, and I could apologize then.

I knew I was too heavy, even with the stronger candle, so I started giving my rice to the cat, Pariji. I wanted to be lighter, light like a little bird. Light enough to fly. Mami didn't notice, she just went through the motions of caring in a daze. It hurt me, but then I realized I would soon see Papi and he would swing me around like he used to.

He would make everything better. I had to wait all day before it was night, and we could release the lights. I bit my lip and it made the waiting easier. Finally after what felt like an eternity I scurried to Mami's bedroom and opened her closet. Inside were the lanterns we were going to use. I replaced the normal candle with the stolen one and lifted it up, racing down the path to the cliff where we release them over the sea. My bones hurt when I ran. I noticed that ever since I stopped eating I would get tired more easily and everything hurt more. But it was worth it to see Papi again.

Mami came down after me, carrying her lantern. I noticed a pocket in the lantern that I had never seen before stuffed full with pictures of two people together, a tie and some pieces of paper with writing on them. As I waited for Mami to come down the path and join the rest of us, I noticed that the pictures were of Mami and Papi. Rage filled me. How could she burn what was his? How could she destroy his memory like it never existed? Mami had written on the side of the lantern in gold ink, "The blood of martyrs protects our children." I didn't know what it meant until Mrs. Fravi beside me whispered to her niece, "This is what happens when good men like Gifarv go to war. They leave behind grieving children and sorrow."

It was then that I truly understood why the lanterns were scarlet. It was blood, the blood of my father and my uncles and my grandfather, who all died fighting a stupid, stupid war. All I wanted to do was see my father again.

Mami leaned down and lit my candle, her eyes alive for the first time in months, glistening with tears. As she released her lantern, I held onto mine. Slowly the lantern started to lift up, but I clung to it stubbornly. Mami didn't notice until my feet lifted off the ground. A thrill of elation flew through me, but she seemed unhappy. Maybe she was just jealous that I would see Papi again and she wouldn't.

"Come back, Fahava!" she screamed. "Let go before you fall!"

I ignored her, smiling and the lantern lifted me higher and higher into the sky. It felt like I was flying, like I would see my father again, he was so close. I could almost feel him hugging me, smiling, his big loud belly laugh that I used to joke made the persimmons on our tree fall off.

It was perfect, so perfect, the moon shining on the water and the lanterns all around me lighting up the sky. I could see Mami on the cliff still, see her mouth moving, but I couldn't hear what she was saying. Then my fingers started to cramp from hanging on. The urge to let go was so strong I almost did with one hand, just to feel some relief, but I stayed stubborn. The higher I climbed with my lantern the less feeling I had until one of my traitorous hands slipped. It fell to my side limply while I struggled to keep holding on. Now I was terrified, all my thoughts about seeing Papi gone. All I wanted to do was get off the stupid lantern and go home to Mami. I knew I could fix her if I tried hard enough. She would truly love me again.

I let go of the lantern.

The fall was exhilarating, the feeling of nothing but air. I fell for what felt like ages until my body hit the water. It was hard like the dirt outside my home, not the soft embrace I had imagined. One of my legs started to hurt. I struggled to climb to the surface. My eyes were open and I could see the sky of red above me, where life waited. But I was weak from not eating and slowly I started to drift downwards. My lungs started to ache so I took a breath in. For a minute everything hurt, it burned even though I was in the water, but then peace came. Papi's face was in front of mine. I smiled. Maybe heaven was at the bottom of the sea, not at the top of the sky.

My last thought was to tell Mami she was sending her lanterns to the wrong place.

## Belly Ache

Help me find the bottom of my insatiable stomach.
I swallowed Black crows in my woman mouth
stored them in the abyss of my gullet.

While swimming through my digestive juices,
I found images of my past selves
breathing underwater
awaiting rescue.

This churning stomach
has always been my familiar misery.
A safe haven for my discarded
female dreams and lonely.

Swallowing sugar cubes
trying to convince my broken body
to remember
we are all sweetness
deserving women.

Through the distance,
I see a brilliant light.
It is the old ancient ones
pointing towards the escape hatch.

They invite me to exit my own belly button
to rebirth myself.
I squeeze my woman self through
the smallest of holes.
I invite the multitudes of my past woman selves
to suction our brined bodies
into our own new beginnings.

Covered in slimy muck and mire
we slide through this birthing space
into the daylight hours
of our own freedom.
Every day,
I drink hyssop root tea and gin
to keep the Black crows nestled in my belly
too drunk to escape.

## Nine-year-old girls

Nine-year-old girls
step on scales,
calculating self-worth
in pounds and kilos.

## MTWTFSS

She weekly wore the same off-season, pastel-colored merino scarf
when she would come for her 3:30 p.m. espresso in the concourse
of the Arts Centre following her Eighteenth-Century Women's
Literature lecture which she taught in the Michelmas term, every
autumn, holding hardback, discolored Haywoods, Burneys, and
Radcliffes up high in the nook of her left armpit, and tucking them
tight to the curve of her ribcage with the pointed nub of her elbow,
back to front, dipping down at the nearest edge, so the black and
white stripes of the library's barcodes would peer out under the dusty
fringed pink, like camouflaged zebras in miniature peeking through,
while she'd deftly maneuver the over-disinfected, acrid-smelling
oblong teak tray lightly along the three-part cylindrical steel rail
with the tips of the fingers on her right hand, pausing individually
at the comely chocolate-dipped strawberries, exquisite macaroons,
mouth-watering bakewells, toothsome apple slices, dainty sponges,
heavenly red velvets, delectable Battenbergs, scrumptious scones,
luscious blackcurrant jam and fiendish clotted cream, only to never
give in to the temptation of a moment melting on her tongue, but to
always resolutely continue on, pick up the tongs and place one lump
of densely packed demerara sugar into her short and squat white with
gold trim demitasse, passing it to me from its gilt-edged saucer, not
trusting the umber Arabica liquid to dissolve the sugar in her cup
unless it was piping hot, straight from the grind and the press and
the pour of the manual machine, waiting with teaspoon ready to stir
it through immediately the second I would hand it back to her, not
stopping until she had sweetened the bitterness all the way through,
holding up the queue with her swirling and twirling, then fussing and
fishing the exact change out of her jacket pocket, because sweetening
was the only thing on her mind, and mine, when I'd weekly store
up questions I'd never ask her, like how foreshadowing she thought
the work of Aphra Behn to women's literature, and what about the
feeling of the vowels of Oroonoko opening her up in ways she'd never
expected them to, the surprise of the undulation of the four syllables
between the consonants, on the cusp of her tongue and the ridge
of her mouth, our unspoken shared knowledge of the necessity for
permission to petition one's object of affection, what was the true

meaning of *Love in Excess*, did she think that ever even possible; while she would walk on to sit at her window seat way too far down the far far end, next to the seemingly endless floor-to-ceiling panes, unwinding her woollen rose wrapping, gazing out at the university forecourt with all the tiers of learning, industry, domesticity and solace folding forwards on each other until they reached the expanse of the bay below. I came to think on that blush scarf as if she had Tuesday sewn into the label, like it corresponded to a specific pair of day-of-the-week knickers. I knew I shouldn't. But I did.

## Free

In this lingering light    of a late winter    against a coral-covered sky.
I have passed forty-two    age my mother was    when she died.

Once so hot-headed,  I strutted no, left home    tearing
remnants of   my childhood umbilicus to shreds   as I rushed
into life   wearing only the clothes on my back.    Free, finally free!

Multicolored messenger bag   hugging her hips   half the size of my
   own.
As I walk out of a movie    a shadowy figure    surges behind me

impatient with my relaxed pace   ear buds blasting   torn-up jean
   wearing.
She is barely polite    as she fidgets behind me    for several floors.

I can feel her desire   to run amongst crowds   in the multiplex.
In this lingering light    of a late winter    against a coral-covered sky.

Multicolored messenger bag   hugging her hips   half the size of my
   own.
She lunges past    down escalator steps    to bound out the door
   free!
I finally release that giggling girl   woman in the Indian  cotton top.

Savor  sweetness of these middle years.   Enjoy vastness of the view.
I envy her flying feet    cascade of braids    in the evening breeze.

## Rising

Black and white photo,
Black and white kitchen,
Mom and I smile
and beat egg whites in the clear glass bowl.
Cream of tartar, vanilla, sugar, flour, salt
wait patiently to be blended together to become
Angel Food cake.
You can almost hear Perry Como singing
"Catch a Falling Star" on the radio.
The fridge hums along.
The oven pre-heats.
All in good time
the cake will rise.

This happy Kodak moment belies the fact
that beneath Mom's
white apron
white blouse
white bra
white skin
in her right breast,
a minuscule cell is stirring.

## The Journey to Four Hours

Your Doula old as sand
Wise as the sea is wide
Brought you into this life
Caught you with her once-smooth hands

She knew you long before all of us
You told her you were ready to leave
It was your time

The long string of hellos to goodbyes
Cascaded in webs of ringing telephones
We poured into the small sparse room
Where you welcomed us
Your tribe for the last time
To breathe you in take whatever we needed

The Doula told us it would be soon.
It had been four hours since you called
Since I gathered everyone near to your bedside
We had made our way to wash your feet
To wash your feet
To hold your hands

To witness the end of your journey
This moment this fork in the road
The bend without your warmth, your laughter
Without the sheer joy you took at each sunrise
Without that sparkling twinkling in your eyes

Steady my heart to the voids that were coming
Anticipate the threadbare days without you
We were not ready
I asked you to call my name
Whisper it in my ear so that I would hear it always

When you had uttered each of our names
And let go of our hands
It was the child who opened the window
Opened the window

You took your cue
And hovered above us before sailing away!
Before sailing away, sailing away

## Abren los pasos

my grandmother has buried
a country in her left knee her capsule
holds an atlas that will disintegrate at death

Wela,
teach me how to pluck
lavender root lily & purple hibiscus
from the garden and lay
them at the foot of the madonna

the praise and besiege of pressing
your lips against an elder's foot
and extract the wisdom of its crossroads

  teach me how to evade language /how to use my tongue as razor
    against the night sky and split
enter the realms /how to use an octave only the spirits can hear

abren los pasos

## The Sparrow

A sparrow alights—
small sprite upon the
vast glass of an outdoor table,
braces legs like sturdy twigs
for the clear chiseled solo
he's composed.

Every stanza trembles through him,
plucks his taut strung pose.
Silvery notes take flight
while he still anchored holds.

And you, my soul—
who, breathless, knows
the stretch of a neck,
the rapid heart flutter,
a throat filled with one
song awaiting answer.

Take courage from
the brazen little bird
who stands alone
and sings.

## Children Cry in Falsetto

last night i plucked cactus from my tonsils
i plucked fruit from the ravine and my tonsils got infected
last night i was plucked, and my fruit was taken
i was taken, plucked feather by feather until i lay bare
i can't bear to walk, my foot is a mine of pus
what is there left to walk?
listen close, hear the wrath of migrant children
can you hear me? migrant children on boats no raft
the boat is too heavy and bodies are anchored
last night, while on the boat i swallowed the sea
the sea is an anchor and swallowed my body
my body is buried beneath land and water
these lands and waters gather children and beg for dirge
have you done that?
forced a melody from the grave?

## Pool Hopping

*The great thing about this country is
we are free to do as we please but if you block the road
I want to drive down I will run you over if you try to stop me
from voting I will take you out! If you try to move
into my house without being invited you will be DEAD.
(Facebook post by a childhood acquaintance, 2016)*

### 1976

Fourteen and free to do as we pleased,
we hopped fences, remember?
When deck lights lit we ducked
in arborvitae shadows,
hid behind boxwoods neatly cubed
by landscape crews, hired for a song.

We dipped in pools that glowed
in the dark, until their owners —
tanned, silky-robed and cock
tailed, razed us with flashlights. Even
as we ran away, their lawns cradled
our smug, bare soles, soft as the plush,
precisely vacuumed room carpets inside.

Memorize this, before we get too old —
Those lucky nights
when Mr. Smith and his flashlight
went back to bed,
we lay in clovery grass, not touching,
but side by side, Levis and t-shirts
dew-damp. Glassy-eyed, Pop Rocks
buzzing our tongues, we marveled
at galaxies behind fireflies; how insignificant
we were.

## 2016

When a boy
runs across your driveway, leave your fear
in its locked childproof cabinet.
His night-swimming will grace
your pool; watch him lie easy on your lawn,
as he savors the Skittles on his tongue, marvels
in the Milky Way and imagines
his infinity.

## Home

1966: brick ranch. It sits at the end of a soybean field, the same field where my uncle's horse contracts rabies and transmits it to my uncle.

1967: one-story apartment building. My next-door neighbor is a single lady with four kids. The youngest is six, same as me, and teaches me how to light and inhale a cigarette.

1968: same apartment building, different unit. This one has a view of an old pool, now filled in with dirt. It also comes with a new boyfriend for Mom.

1970: a tract house. From here, I can ride my bike to the library, where I find a book hidden in the stacks. On the cover is a black man's fist held high in the power sign. I am too afraid to check it out.

1971: same tract house. My new stepfather installs a metal shed to keep the garden tools he uses to manage the half-acre garden he planted. He always wears a straw sun hat, and today, he comes out of the shed with a black widow spider hanging from it by a thread of silk. Tonight, I will draw a red diamond on my belly with a felt marker.

1978: dormitory at Wash U. I sit in the window, cigarette in hand, and listen to Simon and Garfunkel's "America." I dream of Pittsburgh, Saginaw, and counting cars on the New Jersey turnpike.

1980: two-bedroom bungalow on Gaston Street. My roommate is a Madonna fan and always wears a black mini-skirt and fishnet stockings with the feet cut out. I am in my Grateful Dead phase.

1984: a house on Pill Hill in Seattle. Five people all cooped up in one house. Matt is a photographer and follows the grunge band, Mudhoney. Tom reseeds trees after Weyerhauser deforests timberlands. He's missing his right pinky finger. Betsy is from Indiana and works in a fair-trade gift store on University Avenue. She hates her job but secretly loves Tom. Freesia is a beautiful girl from California who'd been nearly eviscerated as a thirteen-year-old while sledding in Tahoe City. I have the attic room with a small window at one end. I position my bed to see the stars on the rare clear night. I pretend to be the Little Princess or Rapunzel, but my hair isn't golden.

1988: a camper parked at the base of Mt. Shasta, California. I come for the Bluegrass Festival and stay for the boy. We eat pie with our hands, drink wine straight from the bottle. Eight months later, I lie on my back in the grass, my belly swollen so big with my child, it blocks my view of the mountain.

1989: a two-room cabin on the edge of Lake Kachese. Me, the boy, and a child named Susanna, nicknamed Bee, because her first noises sound like the inside of a beehive, full of energy. She has the boy's hair—blonde curls. Her smile keeps me going when the boy needs more space and moves to town. I see him later that spring with a girl from the mountain bike shop. I refuse to admire her muscular arms.

1991: an apartment in town. The boy and I are friends. He keeps our daughter while I attend classes. I finish my bachelor's degree, my master's degree, become a therapist. I sometimes see the boy's girlfriends in my office, but I keep my advice professional. I don't tell them to beware the beautiful smile, to deny his hands, which can smooth the roughest places in your soul, to avoid those eyes, deep pools of need to drown in.

2001: a house on Queen Anne hill in Seattle. Home. I chose the house because of the way the early morning fog gives way to a view of Puget Sound. Bee is now short for Beautiful Thirteen-Year-Old Daughter. She calls me by my first name, Cynthia, instead of Mama. She calls her father, the boy, by his first name also. Sam. She has the spirit of an eagle perched to fly. The boy and I drink vodka sodas while she delivers a speech about the perils of not recycling, animal rights, women's rights, human rights, hunger in Africa. We listen patiently as the sun falls behind the house. Finally, the boy says he must head home. He kisses me and Bee on our cheeks. Bee and I stand, arm-in-arm, in the driveway and wave to his taillights, but we stay where we are. This is our home.

## High Tide

Drained, wholly
    broken
picked to the last flesh on bone
When I attempt to cry all that emerges
is salt.
A solid and elemental grief

I wish that mourning lasted
only as long as the sun
that by evening we could be healed
by the baptismal moon
washed holy and stripped of our sorrow

Hearts mended, we could move
forward
like the waves of the ocean
limitless in its cycles
meaning and memory that does
not hold
guilt or shame

but spits them back upon the shore
as driftwood and seaglass memories
recognizable but reborn
charged with the energy of remaking

## Basil Grows from Mother Earth

martyrs turn de town red

Shango Baptists thundering down
Woodford Square in silence
fifty-six days of protest

pow pow pow
        ping
                panning the atmosphere
steel hitting the ground
like Invaders' tenor section
playing de bass rhythm
of *Plant De Land*[1]

Mother Earth had a vision
to shake up de modern world
with its blue guns blazing
told de Earth People
go north to grow Basil[2]

        because Basil was the king of herbs
        because basil people come as indentured servants from
                southern India
        because black people was all o' we sufferers serving dem
        because dey bring dey modern ting to dis Carib land
        because dey bring dey modern ting to dis Arawak land
        because dey force we mout to say "because"
        because dey call dis "civilization"
        because dey call we lazy fo' bu'nin the chalice
        because dey come up nort to shoot we down
        because dey say we runnin' round exposed like African
        because dey say we hair stand tall like trees

but we say Mother Earth
dat is wat we call she
rid she slave name, Jeanette Macdonald[3],
to give birth to her only begotten son
name him Basil 'cause he's king
policeman come and try to shoot him down
but dem doh kno Mother Earth seed
still growing strong

[1]Plant De Land is a calypso/soca song by Lord Shorty.

[2]Basil Davis was a demonstrator who participated in the Trinidad and Tobago 56-day march and demonstrations for racial unity. Basil was shot dead by police officer Joshua Gordon on Monday, April 6, 1970, after he begged the officer to not arrest someone who appeared to be homeless or mentally challenged. The funeral for Basil Davis on 9 April 1970, was transformed into the largest, most dynamic demonstration in the history of Trinidad and Tobago. Over one hundred thousand persons took part in the funeral march from Port of Spain to San Juan (wired868. com). Basil Davis is considered the first martyr of the Trinidad and Tobago Revolution.

[3]*The Encyclopedia of New Religious Movements* described the Earth People as an antinomian Africanist community settled on the north coast of Trinidad which originated in the visions of their leader, Mother Earth (Jeanette Baptiste, 1934-1984). Anthropologist and psychologist Roland Littlewood was allowed to live on the compound and later wrote a book entitled *Pathology and Identity: The Work of Mother Earth in Trinidad*. He detailed diagnosis based on his study which described Mother Earth as having an episode of thyrotoxicosis resulting in a clinical pattern of hypomania and another man having schizophrenia. However, he concluded that the founder and members were subsequently shown to be psychologically normal. The compound where the Earth People resided was attacked and raided by the government and police and on numerous occasions both founder and members were both arrested and mentally institutionalized. The compound was eventually burned down.

## On the Sidewalk

There is so much black smashed flat
a cricket, antennae tracing parallel to the cracks
a banana peel, wasted compost on the stamped cement
a handful of weave, like the world's longest eyelash.
If I was smashed down here,
I'd bleed out red over my chalk outline
but a single day of rain would wash it all away.

## suppression

these are not tears, you see
(because you won't)
this is the sea, like an ocean
held back behind my dammed eyes
I was restrained by your—
quiet suppression
dried up as driftwood beached
but later
I began to leak, creaky old boat
of my body caught in
turning tides, neap tides, high tides
pulled, pulled, pulled by a yellow moon
a moon the size of a six-bedroom house
a moon who never gave up
pulling at tears so firmly
so quietly suppressed,
buried grief toxic, untouchable
(unwantable like me)
like radioactive waste
carted deep into a salt mountain, hidden
but everything
leaks out over time
changes the color of the sea, blooming red:
you cannot hold back the tides

### sanctuary

i found a way to cloister my mind

i shackled all my loneliness   hurts   regrets
in the chamber of no return

today i peacefully live in my memoirs
bathe joyously in my past pleasures

at last i can stoically wait for my end

## Organized Crime

Al was an unattractive man, at least ten years my senior, maybe more. Given to tasteless jokes as it turned out, he had hired me at $50 more a week than I was making with the legislative lawyers. As a single mother, I was more about the money than the status of the ivory office. Still, this was a stretch, but then again, I never seemed to do the same thing twice.

"Soon you'll know so much, I'll have to marry you," he said.

I laughed. It was true I didn't know anything about the truck stop business. So I set out to do the extra it would take to get up to speed. In the office I was in my organizational element. Cleaning up was the order of the day. Old license plates got neatly filed and those small metal strips with numbers on them found a cozy spot in the pencil tray of Al's desk drawer. He wasn't there to ask, but I thought they might be important, so I put them where I thought he'd find them easily—rather than strewn about in unlikely places.

I'd gotten the payroll under control and had met a lot of the mechanics those first two weeks. Coincidentally, I was dating Richard, a trucker with a brilliant mind, broken in the war. He let me know that there was talk about the new girl in the office, but the talk would soon get better.

When I got to work on Monday, the FBI was there. Al had been arrested and they were collecting evidence. Something about stolen trucks—repainted in the night.

"Do they really think I would be that stupid?" he snarled at me out on bail. "Do they think I would keep the VIN plates in my own desk?"

I just shook my head in outraged agreement.

AUDRA PUCHALSKI

## Species

I woke up famous in the gymnasium, in the middle of a lesson
on myself. I made my fortune in performance: falling sadly, falling
joyfully, dripping pleasantly, covered in yellowish plumage.
I woke up inside a rotting log, I woke up on fire, I woke up
being foraged: edible and potable, easy to grow,
prehistoric, melting off a branch of the evolutionary tree,
cousin to the salamander but business casual.
I woke up drowning, I woke up sleeping, woke up extinct
and delicious. The fire does not consume me—I breathe
underwater—my dress twisted between my thighs—
my fur full of embers. I married an axolotl: I made her laugh.
I woke up flying stiff-winged and low over the water,
regenerating limbs, mouth full of screams and ugly songs,
and I will leave a glamorous and interesting fossil.

## Fruit Loop

little circle ohhh
little stranger
sugar oxygen and danger.

ford country squire
locked and loaded
no seatbelt required.

mama pinches our thighs
when we fight
reaches back and grabs
any thigh that is on the right.
sit on the left
we learn early.
sit behind mama.
her pinch twists twirly

the mark is white
with blue edges.

mama drives that big blue boat
with wooden sides
a skimmer
on the wide turns
glide left then right
we lean into each other
then revert back grimmer.

stevie winks then laughs
when the pinch lands on me
he mostly sits behind her
because i forget.
stevie has a bank account
with interest he collects
in the blue bruises on my thigh.

i have my own accounting
when we arrive
and spend my skills when
on cue i cry.
*stevie tripped me* i am pure drama
and pure pleasure as
stevie collects his pinch from mama.

## The Other Life

Before I leave, I want to know
about the other life.

I want to hear my name
from another animal's mouth.

I want to be the tender talons
of coral or the delicacy of a crab's

underbelly. I want to be the blue fish
in the blue ocean—all current and

unhunted. I want shimmer
scales and fins that circle seagrass.

Would I have the same heart?
The same red muscle that pumps

too faintly to hear its own thrashing?

## This World Is Bigger Than Your Broken Heart

Even without enough room
on earth to lay the pieces out

like a jigsaw. Even if their edges
rub each other wrong, like continents

creating earthquakes. Even if your gait
is so wide with sadness, people part

for you on streets. Even if every part
of you pours out like liquid through

cracks that never close. Even if
the cracks show up in the pavements

of your voice. Even if the hollow spaces
make never-

ending echoes. Even if
the emptiness is so large, you can fit

yourself inside it, have it consume you
whole, feet first, a single gulp, blocking

out the sun. Even
if the shards create

a forcefield around you, splintering everything
you touch. Even if your heart is your skin,

your lungs, your hands, your feet. Even if
the wounds grow so large, the light

that enters them looks like darkness
you might drown in. Even then.

# KEN ALLAN DRONSFIELD

## Awaken a Reddish Haze (Pantoum Form Poetry)

Nocturnal shadow, rise with the flamingo
charmed by the sunrise a reddish haze smiles.
Prone upon the pillow cherished teacup pouts
hushed morning sonnet whispers at my window.

charmed by the sunrise a reddish haze smiles
Dreams left to wander my fan begins the day
hushed morning sonnet whispers at my window
humidity now departing the sea birds serenade.

Dreams left to wander my fan begins the day
Sand dunes twinkle like diamonds sparkling
humidity now departing the sea birds serenade
grasses flow serenely terns hover surfside.

Sand dunes twinkle like diamonds sparkling
Mild onshore winds as hot water is now ready
grasses flow serenely terns hover surfside.
a royal blend steeping; cherished teapot grins.

Mild onshore winds as hot water is now ready
My Siamese cat yawns, awake for another day
a royal blend steeping; cherished teapot grins.
the tea tastes sublime; awaken a reddish haze.

## Recherche of "The Windhover" by G.M. Hopkins

Two small boys waiting for the bus early one summer morning saw crows circling above a dumpster. "Bald eagles! Bald eagles!" they were shouting, wild-eyed, enraptured.

Just getting into my car, I was caught between their enthusiasm and my responsibility as a culture-bearer, grand-chief reality checker, teacher, mother. I decided quickly enough to throw facts to the wind and ally myself with wonderment. "Incredible!" I exclaimed, joining the boys. "Wow! Look at that!" And to my amazement, my heart in hiding did begin to stir for those birds. "Morning's minions!" I shouted. "Maybe falcons!"

"Bald eagles!" the kids continued.

"I caught this morning morning's minion," I began to recite with as much drama and abandon as I could muster, "kingdom of daylight's dauphin, dapple-dawn-drawn Falcon, in his riding/Of the rolling level underneath him steady air... " Faltering now, trying to remember how it went so as not to break the rhythm, it didn't matter. Each feeding the other's intoxication, everyone was shouting at the same time. The chant of "Bald eagles" continued.

"Air, pride, plume, here/Buckle!" I whispered, seeing trouble coming out of the corner of my eye. Trailing out of the house, sullen and sleepy-eyed, bare-chested, shirt, shoes, and socks in hand, my twelve-year-old son was descending upon us.

"Look at that, Alex," I waved an ecstatic hand at the sky. "The achieve of, the mastery of the thing!"

"You dorks!" he said in a tone that left no doubt of his authority. "Those are crows. Bald eagles live on mountains. They don't fly in flocks. They don't land on dumpsters. As a starter," he said, giving up on us in disgust, "you can look at their primary flight feathers." He seemed to think that any further instruction was beneath his dignity, and he picked his way over to the car.

"Oh, my chevalier," I intoned, overtaking him from behind, still under the sway of poetry, "Don't you know that there's a bald eagle in every crow?"

"Bald eagles live on mountains," he said. And that ended the matter.

## Origins

*after G.E. Lyon, "Where I'm From"*

I am from skate punk, fuck off, touch my stuff and you die. I am from crystal meth, spoons and needles, paying to get high.

I am from the belt across the back, the fist in my teeth, the polished black hard-soled shoe that kicks me downstairs. I am from waking in vomit, blood and snot.

I am from clay, impervious to pain. I am from stone, never cry no more. I am from dead ash that falls off the end of a reefer and I rub it into my pants leg. I am from the burning cigarette pressed into my skin. I am from the hidden razor, the secret switchblade knife.

I am from a long stretch of asphalt, too stoned to see the end. I am on my bike escaping to nowhere. I am on the side of the road, hitchhiking. I am in the car of a greasy speed freak, going too fast. Ninety mph in under seven seconds, he says. I'll let you ride if you will hold my turtle. —Whatever, let's go, and then the horny shell surprise.

I am from Mad Dog and Thunderbird, puking down my shirt. I am from pot speed and acid, too high to die. I am from the hospital, raving, blood on my hands on my clothes is it mine? I am from four point restraint don't tie me up god please no I can't stand it. I'm from twenty mg. intramuscular Valium jammed in my arm, turning daylight soft and black.

I am from walking, walking the sidewalks of St. Louis, the barrios of Phoenix. Walking the highways of Houston, walking seawalls of the Gulf Coast, walking forests of the Midwest, infested. I am from chiggers and ticks and fleas.

I am from the fires of the Southwest, lightning strikes below the Rim. Late night fire fight red glow smoke choke burns your lungs and your feet blister in your boots. Know your crew in the ash-filled dark by a lock of hair, the looseness of a step. Know your weather, know the wind or die. Two Hotshots burned in the backfire, caught in the draw our own flares created. Burned those boys alive, seventeen and twenty-one, and there was too much smoke and ash to see. The locomotive wind drowns out the screams.

I am from the women: Janie, the dark-haired poet. Dreadlocked Maria, molasses-colored body artist, who threads purple beads in her hair. Elisa, the golden dancer gone to Boulder. Connie, the seeker, and Carole, the listener, and Pat when I write, and Becky who loves me even though I'm sometimes pretty bad.

I am from pen and ink, recreating my life.

## What's in a Box?

This thing showed up at my house today. It's really big. It's square and white, covered in duct tape. I'm confused, but I have to know what's inside. I look for something sharp to get this ridiculous amount of tape off. I finally find a knife to cut away at it so I can see the contents of this mystery box. As I open it, I find myself staring at a familiar face. She looks like me, she sounds like me, but this one is definitely not me. She looks dirty and cold. Her eyes are lifeless, like she has no soul. "Who are you?" I ask her. She doesn't answer. She just stares at me with a blank expression. So I try again. "Who are you?" I ask more forcefully. Nothing. No reaction, no movement, no life. I sigh in frustration. I walk around the side to see who sent this. No one. "What the hell is going on!?" I say to myself. Still not getting answers, just more questions. I walk back around to the front where I opened the box to find it empty. Now I'm even more confused. I look to see no footprints except mine in the snow. She left no sign. Nothing. I put the box in the trash and walk back inside only to find myself on the couch. The same girl in the box, life-less. Flashing, blue, lights. Some people. Mom's crying. I guess it's my fault.

DAVID PONTRELLI

## A Fourteen-Year-Old Girl
## Points Out Her Teacher's Written Comments
## To a Friend

The teacher wrote them shits.

# ANNE DELLENBAUGH

## Oil

I oil my body almost daily.
It's a simple Ayuvedic practice called *abhyanga* in Sanskrit.
In some ordinary way, I think of it as kind
of an anointing or
a daily temple cleaning.

The body that is my gateway
into this world
is also
my lightning rod for spirit.

I'm not sure where to go with this—
not sure how to get where I want to go—
the most, perhaps, horrendous thing that happens
in this profane, ignoble world
is the repeated dis-honoring
of the manifest, the temple.

I want this for every woman—
and yes, man—
but I want for each woman
to know her own body as sacred.
And not even as the vessel of the sacred
but as itself
(an expression of)
Sacred.

## The Garbage Strike

It was the summer I moved to New York City, the summer of the longest heat wave in history, the summer of catastrophic droughts and raging fires, the summer tugboat workers went on strike and trash was left to rot all over Manhattan.

That summer.

The summer the temperature rose to a hundred and one degrees ten days in a row; the summer city sidewalks became nature trails, narrow and sinuous with bulging black bags piled as high as boulders, precariously balanced and quivering as rats—plus-size but agile—bounced from one mountain top to the other.

It was the summer we walked in the middle of the street.

It was the summer my friend Sharon and I went out every night after our shift at Rectangles, the Israeli restaurant at the corner of East 10th Street and Second Ave., where we served pickled turnips, homemade zhug, greasy malawach and sweetened mint tea under Eagle-Eyed Shalom, our ancient boss, bespectacled, half my size, shrunk like a paper ball behind the cash register where he stood all night just to make sure we dumped the leftover pickles back into their old brine before serving them again.

That night, like all nights that summer, it was hot and humid and the streets stank as we made our way east, then south—heading straight for the underbelly of the city—also known as Alphabet City. But first we stopped at Lucy's on First Ave., we stopped at Blue and Gold on East Seventh, we shot pool, we drank shots, we sniffed lines. The sky was purple in that dirty New York City kind of way, in that pollution meets bright lights meets endless possibilities kind of way, and by the time we reached our final destination—Save the Robots, East Second and Avenue B—we felt like we owned that sky even though by that point—that four in the morning point when the real fun began—we already had no money left to buy ourselves the necessary goods for our continued enjoyment, which quickly put us in various compromising situations, as in: Me, behind the locked bathroom door, a line of people waiting outside while this guy I've just met nibbled my neck and dug both hands down my pants; me, again, staring at the moldy blob that sprawled from the toilet tank to the crumbling ceiling, my teeth numbed and that lead taste of freshly inhaled powder seeping down from tongue to throat—Me, even in that state, realizing that a girl needed to draw a line, not just a real line, but a metaphorical line, somewhere, somehow, between what and what—I certainly wasn't in a state to figure out right at that moment, not with customers banging at the door, not with Soul II Soul blasting in the background, not with Sharon temporarily gone—busy, perhaps, in the other bathroom, or scouting out, as only she could do, the top dealer on hand that night.

And then what?

All I know is that wherever I drew that line, I ended up on the side of survival—no complete self-destruction here, just some partial chipping at the edges, a couple of shavings off the core flint that remains and goes on living, hardening.

When we left the bar that morning the sun was already high up in the sky and the mounds of garbage gleamed like volcanic rocks. Sharon and I, reunited at the exit, intact for the most part, zigzagged our way back to our respective apartments, the morning air so dense and humid it stuck to our skin like blood, thick and itching, as if the crust of a scab was already forming.

## A Beggar's Suffering

Her hair is matted to the back of her head,
It's been a long time since she's been fed.
With dirty, worn clothes, she reeks.
It smells as if her bladder leaks.

Sitting on her flattened box,
She shivers from the cold,
Watching as the callous walk by,
Chasing after fool's gold.

Despair resonates from deep lines on her face,
Evidence of her fall from grace.
Ridicule and snickering in her blind-spot,
While the others go by not giving her a thought.

I realize there are those who deceive,
Robbing the kindhearted like thieves.
But you never know what she's been though,
Why from this world she withdrew.

Maybe a loss of a child,
caused her to lose her mind.
Or no medical care,
and her health declined.

A veteran with PTSD,
Or a husband who beat her mercilessly?

Humanity in our society is fleeing,
Where is the compassion for this human-being?

She's not invisible,
She's sitting right there.
Please, just one person,
Act as if you care.
For we all learn eventually,
That life's not fair.

## Rooftop Garden

I've made you another intimate landscape;
a rooftop garden filled with jonquils and daffodils,

graveyard steam and mythic beasts
protected by barbed wire and positronic sentries.

Walking in vacancies of yellow,
I speak in amber motifs mingling in mist

of the difference between captivation and imprisonment,
the similarities of a kiss to a bite on the lips.

All the things we've done to kill each other—
even as our eyes strain, seeking a universal cure,

one more brief world is born of licorice and pity,
abandoned by serpents and gentle crescent wings.

If you feel the pull of a meadow on a distant moon
as I ply a profusion of naked disguises

you may someday believe there is nobility in foolishness,
that withered leaves are orchids in a faraday cage

and that every tiny actuality is a platinum vista meant for us
or occasionally for her, the girl who fell off the mountain.

## Sea Glass

I feel the edges, smoothed by sand over so much time. The clear green that the glass must have been is now opaque, scratched into obscurity by the tide. It's funny how things are never just things. We hold them, touch them, smell them, and they are the keepers of our memory. Of things we thought we forgot. Of things we wish we forgot. This piece of sea glass was the thing I picked up from the beach on the day of summer vacation I realized my father was an alcoholic. This piece of sea glass holds the beginning of the end of my childhood.

I don't know why I kept it. It's not out for viewing. It's tucked away in a box with pictures of the person I used to be. I almost never see it, or think about it. But when I go back to look at pictures and I see it, I know exactly what it is. I can hear the waves and feel the sun on my face as I run down the beach with it in my hand.

Navigating the warren of beach umbrellas, I find ours but there's no one there. I look around and see my mom and dad. They're with a man. The man has my dad in handcuffs. My mom is crying. People are staring. They don't come back for me. They don't even turn around. I start to cry but I'm embarrassed so I lie on my towel, hiding my face in my hands. A man comes over to me.

"Were those your parents?"

"Uh huh. Why did the man take my dad?"

The man sighs. "He was drunk. He was fighting with your mother and shouting at other people."

I looked at him, confused. His eyes showed the realization that I didn't understand "drunk." He looked so sad. At the time I didn't know he was sad for me, not for some nebulous adult reason. Sad at my life. He must have known what lay ahead for me. He excused himself and I watched him walk over to his blanket where his own wife and children were. They were all staring at me.

He turned to his wife and I heard him say, "They just left her here alone. What kind of people. . .?"

I looked in my hand and turned the piece of green glass over in it, studying it very closely. Pouring my memory into it without knowing.

## Home

It's dark. I smell wood and dirty, wet earth. There's something holding me but I'm blind. Even when I open my eyes I see blank, darkness. I try to scream but my voice comes out silent. I seem to be paralyzed. What is going on here? I try to fathom what could possibly be going on. I hear crying. No! I think, Don't leave me here! The sound slowly gets harder and harder to hear. Come back! I scream in my head, but of course, no one can hear.

Still dark, still pinned, still paralyzed. Why? I ask myself. I just want to go home. Please, take me away.

Small light starts to form. It gets bigger and bigger. So blinding! my thoughts say. Home.

## LAWRENCE WILLIAM BERGGOETZ

### Haloed

The words were spoken as if from a lost canon of holy books.
Statements only become philosophy when they impugn the sacred.
Stillness began to define the air; the sun was merely backlight
   through haze;
and the quietness drifted into something closer to a cadence a lute
   would
have once played in a summer courtyard late on a Sunday afternoon.

There is something we cherish which we cannot quite define: an
   exultation
which lasts long after its peak experience, like a sun which will
not succumb to twilight and remains harbored in the mid-afternoon
sky, the clouds having carried their labor far from the bleached azure.
Our happiness seems to collapse before we can manipulate the course
of its rising. Joy exists in vertical moments, while melancholy lives in
   circles.

Random appears the route we travel when we glance back after
   decades.
So many twists along the journey could have landed one so far from
what now seems destiny, while the path feels purposeful for the pain
it evoked. Yet, not everyone finds wisdom; it is realized only by those
who learn how to climb the sky one star at a time all the way to the
   moon
before returning each morning with a voice haloed with darkness.

## Hannah

Under her breath she muttered
prayed, groaned, grunted, sighed
dribbled a stream of pain
over a bed of disdain.

Swift-running sighs
tumbled over barren rocks.

Hannah gushed drunken sounds
in the temple of Shiloh
poured out torrential pain
until her scoured tear ducts
cleansed of dejection
dazzled hope with pain.

## Weight

Make me an anchor.
The weight I carry
keeps slipping.
Forge the links of
anger, fear, and shame.
Let the clasp be of remorse,
so it binds itself to me forever.
Let forgiveness never find me here,
so I live in infinite regret,
undeserving of oblivion.

## Ten to No

It never ends.

The wave of humanity that crashes into this hall may recede by the end of the day, but it resurges with the weight of the moon. By morning, the incoming tide has dredged up the sludge, sullied the waters, and dumped the dregs on our shores. The stench is unbearable, all sweaty and dank.

I have to listen to their stories. It's part of the job. I nod once in a while, tick the appropriate boxes on the requisite forms, but my thoughts fade without fail to my next cigarette. That sweet scent of escape always clears the air, cleanses my palate, and immerses me in a world that doesn't reek of desperation. Today I think I'll forgo the filter to make sure nothing stands between me and my God-given right not to give a shit about anything. By the time the next family walks up to my window, I'm already wrapping my mind in a swirl of mental smoke, fumigating my soul, forgetting the crowds I am tasked with turning away. Above my head time ticks on. The clock is unforgiving. Each new applicant gets a ten-minute countdown to no. The old man standing in front of me keeps glancing at the clock as if it makes a difference.

He doesn't get it.

They never do.

They're all actors in a play that has already been scripted. They arrive on cue from some war-torn hellhole in a sandpit shit place, and they're cast accordingly. I didn't write the play. I can't change the script. But sure, I'll feed them their lines if it helps.

"What about my children?"

They always ask about the children.

"In order for male applicants to be considered children, they must be younger than twelve."

I slide the application across the desk and point to the fine print. Applicant 223 fumbles with his glasses and lifts the page to his face, scouring the script for an alternate ending. He won't find one. There was an applicant 223 yesterday, and another the day before. Why would this one think his lines would be any different?

When the application settles back into place on my desk and applicant 223 looks up slowly (they always look up slowly), I point to the clock above my head. He refuses to look. Instead, our eyes lock. His iris is tobacco brown. Wispy filaments swirl around the impenetrable space that separates his soul from a blood-lined sea of whiteness, but no smokescreen can protect him.

And neither can we.

The clock strikes no, and I slide the frosted window closed that separates me from the churning sea. The packet of cigarettes is already in my hand, liberated from the shadows of my desk drawer, ready and eager to do its job. A cloud of smoke slips into the room as I pull the door open to go. I smell its freedom. I inhale its escape. I follow the dim lights in the veil of the cloud and pull out my lighter to join them.

## Me

I believed I was the *me* she said I was
each time she told the tale.
Because I was five and she was Mom,
the truth was secret, hidden, and frail.
I wore that me like a shield.
It made me feel brave.
I felt it had power I could wield.
When she tried to hurt me, I thought
I could make her see she shouldn't bother.
But like a curse, it spilled from her lips,
"Jesus, you're just like your father."

## Her Kind

The phrase rolls over and over in my mind.
Repeat, repeat, repeat.

I am her kind.
I am so tired of this repeating theme. One after another,
one more sister becomes one of our kind.
The kind that has not been treated kindly. They portray us as the
    misfits,
the ones who make too much of nothing,
who asked for it,
who dressed the wrong way,
walked the wrong path
Should've known better.

But we know our kind:
we are simply women living in a world
where those who live free
exert their will
with little fear of reprisal.

We know our kind; we are strong of soul,
made stronger by the tear in the fabric
that we have so carefully woven over by each other's hands.
They think we are weak, but we know that in the end
we'll not be ashamed, we will have forged the path
for others to follow, where we are no longer silent
Where our truth will reign.

## Feelings Feel

A shovel squeezes between bits of earth
A foot slips into a shoe
Nuts screw onto long, thick bolts
A collar snuggles around a dog's neck
A worm slithers back into its safe hole
This closely and more we align with our feelings.

As poignant as lemon meringue is
And salty chips peck at our taste buds
Crisp, cold ice stings the tongue
Stark boiling tea melts receptive throats
These clearly we know, but so quickly escape
A description

## Italian Excavation

In Grade Nine she read *I Claudius*
In Grade Six, *The Eagle of the Ninth*,
But in Grade Three, she read about Pompeii
buried beneath molten lava and
volcanic ash

she read how archeologists unearthed people
frozen in their daily lives
fossilized forever
by disaster's sudden flow

they even found the form of a dog
caught running
a stolen cake with raisins
clutched in its mouth

In her 20s the rain of ash began
career, marriage, another marriage,
child bearing, child rearing,
another career, and especially work,
always more work

gone were the delicious evenings
of voracious reading
in pleasurable curiosity

her private unwinding thoughts
smothered in family, sociality
choked with constant company

now on retreat in Italy
mere miles from Vesuvian fire
her stolen mornings are spent in silence,
she reads all she wants before bed
and each day her pen
excavates the fossilized, skeletal self
somewhere down below
she knows
a raisin cake lies waiting

CARL BOON

## Richmond at Night, 1864

It's easy to confuse the trees
in the woods beyond, easy to be
struck down, wake up wounded
and thirsty, your trousers
pierced. Ghosts are everywhere,
glaring at you from columns,
from the warm wood of taverns
on Carey Street where they sip
bourbon and listen to the magpies.
You walk past the Hard Shell,
a map tucked in your elbow,
and a dog, shameless and ancient,
growls at you from Jeff Davis Blvd.
He can't see your face,
but he knows you're a foreigner
by the cut of your jacket,
the way you seem dissatisfied.
Even the coins in your hands
seem different, too heavy,
a burden to carry. You were brave
to come here. You were brave
to be enveloped by time.

## A Silver Maple

Hermann remembers the silver maple in front of the house. "Of course," he thinks, "it hasn't been mine for almost fifty years. But that tree was special. It was as if we were married. There were good times and bad times. Mostly good times, I'd say."

He had been gone from the Cities for thirty years. Then he offered to take a lateral promotion at the large company where he worked. He explained to his manager, "I think I've climbed high enough. Set down some strong roots in the Cities: both my kids born there. Kind of like to go back."

Both of his children were now grown up with families of their own and lived in California. Hermann didn't think that should matter. "Let the company think what they want. None of their business anyhow."

His hearing had worsened the last five years. He had lived on his own so long that often he couldn't remember if he had said something to himself or just thought it. He suspected that if he "heard" something clearly, it probably meant he had thought it and that was why it was so clear.

Two years ago, he felt his strength flagging and went for a physical. They ran tests, did some blood work, and then sent him down to the Mayo Clinic for more tests. They gave him the good news and the bad news. He moved into an assisted-living facility.

Two months ago, the bad news started on its final lap. He was now putting his "shit" together. The pain meds he had been using were losing their effectiveness.

Hermann revisits his bucket list. Scratched near the top are two barely legible words: silver maple. He must have written them down after a double dose of meds. "What the hell did I mean by that?"

There is an aide in the room who looked up from what he was doing and asked, "What?"

Hermann is surprised, didn't know he was talking. "Oh, I'm trying to figure out what I meant when I put 'silver maple' on my bucket list."

"Lots of nice old silver maples in St. Paul where I grew up by Macalester College near Summit and Snelling."

Hermann closes his eyes. "I lived west near the University of St. Thomas. Our kids went to Groveland Park Elementary School. I drove through a couple years ago. The buildings are still there, look better than me."

He lies back in his hospital bed. The aide comes over to check. "How you doing, Hermann?"

Hermann squints at the nametag. "As well as can be expected, Jim. There was a big silver maple in our front yard forty years ago. Wonder if it's still there. Didn't feel up to driving past my house when I was in the neighborhood. Now I kind of wish I had. Going to need to close my eyes for a while."

Jim asks if there's anything he can do to make Hermann more comfortable. Jim puts a glass of water on the nightstand and adjusts the blinds. "I'll come by in an hour to check. The buzzer's by your right hand if you need help. Have a nice nap."

Jim writes up a request and sends it on.

Easter comes and goes; April becomes May, and Hermann's condition worsens. They decide to move him into the hospice care wing as soon as a bed is available.

The facility publishes a list of upcoming birthdays the middle of every month. Jim is going down the list and sees Hermann's name. Damn! Never got back to me.

He takes the list and rushes off to the office of the managing director. He stares down the secretary. "No, I'm afraid this won't wait. I put in a request two months ago and it seems no one really cares about our residents. Now one of them is going into hospice care. I'll just stand here until you let me in. And I can see Dr. Marcy is not on the phone."

"If you'll sit down a minute, I'll go in and tell Dr. Marcy that you are waiting. Who did you say this was about?"

"I didn't. It's regarding Hermann Wendell. He's been with us for more than a year."

The secretary comes out five minutes later and says, "You may go in now."

Jim was meditating, breathing rhythmically, and letting the built-up anger flow out of his body. He stands, smiles, and says, "Thank you."

He mentions the request he put in two months ago and the fact that Hermann's condition has worsened. "I'd be willing to go along with him to visit his old house. Off the clock. He has good days and bad days. We'd need less than an hour there and back. It'd mean a lot to him. To me, too. I grew up with big silver maples, and they are special."

Dr. Marcy apologizes. "I'm sorry your request got lost. I'll make sure we find out what happened and put things in place so it won't happen again. Meanwhile, let me check with legal. I don't see any reason why he can't sign himself out for a few hours. And I've discretionary funds that can be used for his transportation. No reason you should have to do this on your own time. We'll schedule it when you're here. As you said, shouldn't be more than an hour. Come by tomorrow at two. I'll let you know what we've come up with then. And thanks for bringing this to my attention."

Without thinking, Jim brings his hands to his breastbone, bows slightly, and says, "Namasté—thank you."

Dr. Marcy smiles. "Namasté, Jim."

Three days later a handicap van drives Hermann and Jim to his old home. There's a look of contentment on Hermann's face. Jim leans over and hears Hermann say something about his kids teasing each other about being a cretin and never going to Princeton like their Uncle Wally. Hermann struggles to explain. "We lived near Cretin and Princeton."

"You rest, Mr. Wendell, no need to explain. We'll be there in ten minutes."

Hermann directs them to a small stucco house on the north side of the street. "That's my old house, but I don't see the maple. Wish I could go out and walk up those steps one more time."

"Let me go out instead. I'll look around."

Hermann moves, moans, and whispers. "The tree used to be up there, near where they have that ornamental gas light."

"I'll check. Maybe I'll see the stump, maybe there're some suckers coming up. That often happens when you take a tree down. It goes on living."

Jim walks up on the lawn, searches for signs of the old tree, and then goes over to the pair of saplings set back closer to the house.

He returns to the van with a broad smile across his face. "Well, Hermann, I've got some good news and some bad news. Bad news first. Couldn't find any signs of that old tree. The grass around the lamp is in the same bad shape as the rest of the lawn. Good news: it looks as if they've planted two new maples in closer to the house. Guess they're about five years old, so they survived at least one of our winters. I gave each of them a kiss from you. You got naming rights."

Hermann smiles. "Thanks, Jim. How'd you know I have two kids? We can write them when we get back to the home. I'm sure they'll be glad to hear the news. They promised to come out and visit this summer as soon as their kids are out of school. Maybe we'll all go back to the old house. Last item on my list. Can't thank you enough."

Hermann dozes off on the way back to the home. The following week a hospice bed becomes available. He passes on the day before Memorial Day. His children come out for the funeral. Jim was not able to get the day off.

## A Branch Like Poetry

Remember the maple tree, the one we cut down last winter after a windstorm dropped large branches into the yard next door barely missing their house, their car, and smashing their fence? The tree, dry and thirsty inside its core, tried to suck water from the earth around its trunk, bony arms reaching and stretching across the garden; plants did not grow beneath it with no water to drink, rotting matter and hardened dirt gathered at its base. From the neighbor's view, she was dying. But that was not what we saw gazing lovingly out our back-porch window in spring. True, she was nothing like the sweet-scented weigela by the front steps greeting visitors engorged with pink blossoms and more pleasing than her perfumed companions lavender, jasmine, evening primrose, geraniums and honeysuckle... easy to love. Our maple had one low-hanging branch we called *like poetry* that carefully arched over the well-trodden path. We sat beneath it, sometimes in despair or when the unrelenting scorching sun burned through us, we took comfort in her leafy embrace, surrounded by her twigs and branches, replete with musty smells of forest decay. But that winter day, we gave permission to chop her down, mercifully removing her feeding and breathing tubes.

Later, we sat on the stump remains, holding vigil, wishing her well in the afterlife.

**For Susan**

Ireland was reflected in her eye
the craggy shoreline
the moon coloring the clouds

The edge of the breeze prickled my skin

She would go to be alone
walk miles in the fields
scramble over stone walls
feel her roots in the rocks

Now, more than ever

Ireland's her safety hatch
she'll go for however long it takes
weeks, months, a year

You'll show me Ireland, right?
I ask her today

She wants her ashes in Dublin
or maybe Sligo.

## Bones (A Sonnet)

To completely clean a bone is hard if
you're not a dog. Gristle clings, scraps hang on.
Bones have pride. Leave one out and fuzz will grow.
Scrub it with alcohol—that makes no dent.
Bones, like shells, are hard to crack. Suck on it now.
Extract the marrow. It'll cure you or
hasten your demise. Bury your bones for
a hungrier day, for a hungrier day
is on the way. Boil your bones for soup.
They'll break down. In the Donner Party,
ox bone soup went by the name of Pot of Glue.
The bone moves in the socket until it
doesn't. No glue can fix it. Bone on bone,
skeleton under the skin. Ossified.

## what if I wish for a storm

what if I wish
and the sky so large
as it is on this side—

the sky storms
with grey and purple
and scatters of blue

light streaking through a painting
from the Hudson River school
perhaps wind over gold sand
lonely main illumination

what storm isn't
    and the rain
    and the rain (listen to the rain)
the desert torrent
charging upon us
cleansing—I like the wind best—
and water on dry earth perfume

making a person
breathe deep to catch some
it only smells like that sometimes
above snakes and wildflowers
over alkaline waters
through a canyon

wind that screams in caves
while fish jump on the way to the dam

## My mother is trying to tell me something

but only blackbirds fly from her lips.
Her eyes hollow like twin moons,
hair long, long, long shut fast
in the window frame and
I push, push, push but
I can't get her free
so I cut it, gray
lock by gray
lock.

## SUHALY BAUTISTA-CAROLINA

### Ese Trapo En Tu Cabeza

My mother called me today to tell me que se soñó con mama
su mama, mi abuela.

In the dream, my grandmother is wearing a scarf on her head. This
    scarf is something we have in
common, my grandmother and I: the covering of our heads.
This is what my mother has always told me.
Beyond breath and time, we are connected.

In the dream, my mother tells mama how beautiful her headwrap is,
    the same way she tells me;
she wishes she could wear one like I do. She wishes. I am filled with
    my mother wishing.
She always asks me how I do it; how I can tie the fabric so gracefully,
    so confidently into a
glorious crown.
I always assure her that she can do it to herself too.
I promise to teach her, but I haven't.

Recounting the dream. This is something we always do.
Tradition.
Habit.
The way we speak to each other without getting too deep.

I try to envision mama—the only way I can imagine her, from the
    black and white photo of a
photo that I own where she is dancing with my uncle—the only one
    of my uncles I call "tio."
She is dressed in all white, her sainthood demanding the viewer's
    complete attention. I obsess
over the parts of her face that evidence my mother. I think about
    the way mama would have loved me, with the same stern love my
    mother coated me in from birth, or from before birth.
I can't remember but I know.

In the dream, mama tells my mother to "wait right there" or probably,
    "esperame ahi."

I move mama in my mind
the way I want her to move
floating.

Mama comes back to the same spot where she left my mother. In her
    hand is the delicate, pear-
colored scarf that I bought for my mother in Verona last summer. She
    ties it effortlessly onto my
mother's head, making the glorious crown my mother has been
    longing for.

LISA FAVICCHIA

## All of This Is About Lifeless Eyes

Have you ever perfectly mimicked
the camel spider?
It's like a body
if a body were like glass
and you could see yourself
swirled up inside a conch,
then every morning shed,
put on your flesh
costume, carefully tuck
and stitch any protruding
sphagnum moss.
Only you will ever know
that you're see-through,
that part of you thinks
not all legless lizards are snakes,
that you could have fuzzed antlers
if only someone understood rippling fur,
or that these eyes are alive eyes
and they made you afraid to touch.

## The Heart Stone

If some dawn, that I wake:
With disappointments from the night,
That brought my heart aches—
I will reach not for the lover,
Whose love was ever so cold,
But for you, Rose Quartz,
Whose heart chakra vibration:
Can tender and soothe its very rhythm,
And I will hold it there—
To recharge its energy,
And to renew its faith,
Making my heart whole again.

DUDGRICK BEVINS

## Before Your Absence Had a Body

There was no body
But we couldn't bury your casket empty,
So we rebuilt you in birds.

I found a fallen sparrow,
Wings broken,
With no nest above,
And I laid him on the silken pillow
Where we should have
Laid your head instead.

Your brother and father
Each grieving in his own way,
Wrung the neck of a bantam rooster
To give you boots of rainbow
And of gold:
This, a simple reference to your cowboy days—
The childhood as intangible now
As your face.

Your mother,
In a fit of rage,
Took your rifle from its case—
The one she didn't want to buy you
When you were twelve
But did anyway—
And sat in silence for two whole days...
The desert wind
Her only company
Until the eagle was overhead.

She took its carcass
And folded in each wing
So as to give you a torso—
A rib cage—
A place to lay her head and weep:
Weep the wretched cries
She couldn't speak before
Your absence had a body.

## Confession #19
*for Ryan*

When his fake was taken and tossed on the table
with a curt goodbye, I knew the smoke would crawl into his lungs
as he stoked the anger with American Spirits.

We talked about anger a few weeks after, understanding
people paint emotions with only the primaries:
sad, mad, glad.

Maybe if we had the words for feeling the way we do
for color, we wouldn't see ourselves as paint-by-number, but
as Pollock meets Picasso, splatter cubism, the kind of art I would at
    least admit to misunderstanding.

Instead we storm down Duval Street
looking at the shops and the drunken smiles through the red tip of
    the lighter
and tell ourselves we are this one shade
and maybe if we pull enough black into our lungs we can close our
    eyes
and the world will be dark enough to sleep
without crying.

GOPAL RAMAN

## where the haze tells the horizon to stop

a heavy cloud sits, slowly, at the corner of my
sight, vision muffled by tumbling gray weight.
the trees, they say, sparked and spit its skin

to these skies. but even i know the smoke sleeping
in my winds wasn't from a foreign forest. no, the
roots that shed this smog grew in grass that i

had once known. the trees, now this scattered,
airborne ash, held in tight embrace the same soil
that brought me into this world. i wasn't born

a lonely, little being—no, i was born a brown,
knotted, immense mess of root and vine,
of story and struggle, of bud and ash. the cord

from my belly ran through my mother to hers,
from hers to hers, and on and on until growth
became ground. stem sucking from mother's

root, fluid flowing from dirt in all ways hidden from
sense. i sipped, teeth barely poking out of brown
gums, from that same spring, that same runnel

that etched soul into my song. and the soul, in
turn, gave my sight only the whisper of what its
older voices left behind. i still long to see what

pushed my teeth out from their home, who whispered
to my roots to leave the soil, what current carried the
saplings away to a less forgiving and familiar land.

i know now i miss the dirt. my voice cracks for
want of home. not for house of concrete and
burning bulb but for home of steaming kitchen

and crunchy popcorn gravel. i've been a plant potted
for travel since birth, and terra-cotta fists hold fast
around my neck, slowly twisting and twisting and

twisting. i long for a sky clear enough to see the end.
i long for this smog to crack open before me. i long
to return to where i can stretch my roots and feel

warmth, not just wall. a dead, scratched paper
says i belong, but even i know no bleached corpse
can offer my bark and bones a forest of my own.

the horizon shimmers unseen behind this haze,
and the forest fires rage all around. smoke smothers
the smells of what my past knew once as breath.

but that air is there no longer. alone, i bend my back
to drink from this foreign stream and to overflow
my terra-cotta world. the horizon across the

oceans belongs to a warmer past, one whose only
witness now sails the smoky skies. but i close
my eyes, sight now lost to smog, to taste what

i can no longer see. this is what an ancestry is, isn't it?
sense blended into self, the way this taste becomes
tree, the way the past becomes present only in me.

## Growing Pains

I shouldn't be here. I know I shouldn't. But I tried to stay in bed as long as I could and the pain will not go away.

I don't usually do this. I shouldn't be here. They're sleeping, I know, and we all have school tomorrow and work and I have to go back to swim practice again. But my legs hurt. A lot.

I tap on the door, softly.

No answer.

It's pretty dark, but I can see my bare toes. It's cold. I can't feel the cool brass doorknob to my parents' bedroom. I'm never supposed to come here unless it's an emergency. It's a wood door, I know, because I watched the carpenter install it to the brass hinges when he built this much-needed addition to our house.

Maybe if I sit down here the pain will go away. Wait, my face is wet. I'm apparently crying? Oh no, my brothers better not see me. They will just laugh and call me the worst name....they'll call me a girl.

I don't know what to do.

I tap then curl my knuckles up, reaching for courage to deliver a little harder knock. I'm not faking something like my little brothers do with their numerous stomach aches. This is real. Will they be mad at me?

O.K. I'm second oldest of the five so I should be able to take care of myself at age twelve. But I don't know. This hurts. I wish my aunt was here.

"Who's there?" His voice. Dad's voice.

"It's me," I say. "My legs hurt bad, very bad. I'm sorry, but it hurts."

"Go back to bed." She is awake now. "It's just growing pains. You're a big girl now. Just go back to sleep."

I whimper. I slide down to the floor. I cry more, very, very softly.

Then I pick myself back up off the floor and begin the painful barefoot walk back to my room, and I close my door.

I push most of my stuffed animals off my bed. They can't help me now. My legs still hurt.

How hard it is to grow.

Even more, how hard it is to be ignored. I need to learn to swallow my pain, no matter how much it hurts and learn to ignore it as though ignoring it would make it disappear.

I'm a big girl.

## Two-Faced River

The water can rise, the water can fall
The river can be kind; the ocean can be merciless
Waves may caress your feet as you step in
Or lash out with violence over dunes and levies

Rushing, pouring
Down the drain or over a roof
Harmless and tame
Or with enough power to crush man's artificial cave

The river can carry you to places unknown
Whether it's peacefully on a boat
Or clinging to driftwood
Torn from the fence of your home

You can roll up the legs of your pants
Shed your shoes and gently wade in
Or be caught and thrust downstream
With the force of being struck by a moving machine

A river carries many meanings
Too many stories to count
Even each leaf, fluttering from a tree branch
Into the water and the waves
Travels a different path down the same river

## Soul Sisters

The heavy winds of the dry season swayed the trees in an endless rocking in the forest land. In the savannah it parched the grass to crisp straws. When Kupuuzwa* walked through her chimp clan, her dragging wrists attracted brambles and straws to her jet fur. She needed a friend for grooming.

Others already etched her snout jagged with the scars of her expulsion. They glowed bright on her dark face at dusk. No chimp female would touch her tonight, no grooming of acceptance ever came her way. So she limped on the ground between the trees looking for a warm spot to sleep. Dry season days are hot, but desiccated air is thin and cold at night, colder than the shoulders of all her kin. When she found a bare patch of ground that fit her curl, she lay upon it alone and slept, a dreamless existence.

In the morning no dew clung to the surrounding grass stalks, but a liquid blue knee blocked the sun from Kupuuzwa's face. She awoke. Her eyes fluttered under her arching brow, curved like a roll of wet clay before a pair of hands could work it into a pot handle or something more useful than Kupuuzwa was to her clan. In the diffused sunrise she sat up to see a naked arm resting on a knee, the hand outstretched, but hanging calmly. The white tipped finger swayed over the fur on Kupuuzwa's arm and did not pull away. A lump like warmth rose in Kupuuzwa's throat and burst like a yawn—relaxed and welcome.

Kupuuzwa reached out her ebony nails to gently rake them through the woman's hair. The strands opened ashen furrows exposing the white of her scalp, and Kupuuzwa's mouth opened again to the round of a chimpanzee smile. Her brow lifted and she looked through each furrow. Kupuuzwa weeded this pewter garden of hair before she finally turned her back to the woman, sat nearly in her lap awaiting the spotted and wrinkled hands to groom her, too.

The woman's lined eyes cast down, but not without mirth. She knew the eyes of an outcast and the gratitude of touch. The day her sister stopped combing her hair on the lace-ruffled twin bed still remained in her lacerated heart. The barrettes and bobby pins of her youth could not hold the sisters together. So today, she rescued a neglected soul from the loneliness of eternity by pulling one straw at a time and flicking it to the earth.

*Kupuuzwa means neglected in Swahili

BRAD JOHNSON

## The Tail

My daughter's favorite film is Disney's *Little Mermaid*,
which I'm afraid instructs her the point of her existence
is to marry and to accomplish this she must sacrifice
her identity, give up her fin, erase her voice from the equation.

After years of listening to her beg for a mermaid tail,
after swimming lessons and proving she can tread
in the deep on her own for minutes at a time, my wife
and I concede, surprise her with one for her seventh birthday.
She immediately pulls it on and hops to the car
like a real mermaid up the beach after a scrambling crab.

The older girls at our local pool swarm my daughter
on the steps, adoring her as if she arrived on half shell.
Every compliment they pay her: *It's awesome; so cool;
I'll trade you for my little brother* she accepts personally.
She describes the process of selecting the blue and green scale
pattern, demonstrates how the triangle of industrial plastic fits
in the fabric below her feet to power her butterfly kick.

On the other side of the pool, two girls lean against the wall.
The girl with pigtails mumbles how my daughter should
be embarrassed of all this attention as the other girl swims
away to join the others at the altar of my mermaid daughter,
leaving the pigtail girl to pout like a celebrity abandoned
by fame. The pigtail girl paddles to the deep end and climbs
the ladder slowly like some new weight's been added
to her suit. She tells her parents she wants to go home
before lifting a towel to dry off, starting with her legs.

ALEXANDRA SMITH

## Sketching at the Circus

They reach toward stars they cannot see
in the world that exists
only under the big top.
Acrobats balance on wires,
and dangle from rainbow silk
while artists sketch them.
Intertwined in a graceful arch,
magic movement flies off the page.
Pen on paper meets power in air.
Lines and shapes flow together,
bodies synchronize, strength meets grace.
A ballet in flight, sailing through the air,
floating for just a moment,
lingering high above
under the big top.

### Resilience

These boots, scuffed and weathered,
have traversed miles fraught with
challenges. Yet every unfamiliar landscape—
every fresh face—pries a broken
heart's vault open a little bit more.

And leather, once parched and cracked,
is painstakingly oiled and polished.

Refurbished soles move onward in
search of an ever-elusive place
to call home, a place to finally
nourish sturdy roots, carries on
steadily in contemplative silence.

## Whisper

Like static on the raindrops,
cool and electric I almost hear you
but you are so far away.
I hear a whisper and
I strain to listen. I try to hold on but
still so far away.
I sit here waiting
breath caught in my chest
almost a sigh this time.
I know there's something
but it is still so far away.
I take a breath and as I release
I open. I must listen.
A small voice rides on a gust of wind.
I know this is important
and I must listen
But it is still far away.
I curl up tight and hold myself close
and remind myself again
today is not the day.
I will once again wait
for the someday when you call my name.

## Green Baby

Before my wife and I were married, we were out driving one day to get roti. It was the weekend, just before the start of a clement Long Island summer. We had just passed the urgent care center and had started downhill toward the highway. She sat with her hands in her lap and was staring out at the trees when she said she was worried about her eggs.

I reached over and gave her fingers a squeeze.

"I think he in some kind of trouble," she said.

I nodded in that instinctive way I do when I'm driving or slicing vegetables or writing a note and want to acknowledge what she's said even though I haven't actually processed it yet. "Wait," I said, coming to. "What do you mean?"

"I dreamt about him."

"About who?"

"My ex."

Ex. Right. "Oh."

"What you think I said?"

"Nothi—I wasn't sure. I didn't hear you right. What happened with him?"

"Well, it was you, me, and my cousin Sherman, and we were back in Dominica. It was night, and we were standing on the lawn, and my ex he come runnin' up. And he was naked, in that he had only a shirt on, but only one arm was through, you understand? The rest of his shirt was just hangin', you know. And he was hard." She gestured with her fist. "And he don't say nothing. No hi, good night, no good to see you. No words to you or to Sherman. He just cryin.' Tellin' me how sorry he was, dat he knew he'd hurt me, dat I didn't deserve it, and dat he want me to give him another chance, you understand?" She cleared her throat, rubbed the front of her neck with her fingertips. "And so I calm him down, I say hold on. I took di shirt and tied it around him to cover him up and took him around to da side a di house. And he start sayin' it again, dat he was sorry and all a dat, you know. But I took him, right, and I held our foreheads together. I said it's okay. He didn't have to feel bad anymore. We had our time and it was bad sometime, but it was in di past. And I was okay. I'd found someone and I was in love, and we were going to start a family."

We stopped at a light and I took her hand. I asked how he had responded to that.

"He said he felt better. But not really doh. I doh think he really felt better. I think he goin' through something. Most times when people naked in my dreams it's because they havin' some kind of problem. Some crisis. It like they been stripped, you understand? Like he ah been stripped of his dignity."

I nodded, and I thought of her sitting perfectly still weeks before while Dr. Wu tried to explain unexplained infertility. "Your follicles don't appear to be working properly," she had said. "If your body can't produce mature eggs, then the only possibilities are to use a donor or a surrogate. Either way, you'd need eggs from another woman."

In the car, she looked at me in that large-eyed, loving way she does when she knows my mind has drifted elsewhere. "Green Baby," she said, and brought me back. The light had changed. I started driving again, and she continued. "I won't be surprised if I call back home to check on him, if I call his uncle or his cousins and find out he in trouble."

She always stunned me like that. He didn't deserve her compassion, let alone absolution. This man had done unspeakable things to her, physical and emotional things, so much that I'd reckoned it a blessing he and I had an ocean between us. I knew in that moment that she was the most mature human being I'd ever met, and I cursed nature for its indifference. As I turned the car onto the highway, I asked if she would call.

"No," she said. "If he call, he call. I not his mother."

## Breakwater

Down the road from Cannon Square,
Take a right toward the harbor,
Traverse the uneven stones,
Laid by man and rocked by storms.
The jetty stretches out,
Taking the brunt of rough waves,
Protecting the boats and docks
That lay in Stonington's bosom.
Out on that row, one with the ocean,
One forgets the faults of land.
A lonely boat passes in the night
With a searchlight in front,
The last to come in from sea,
Hoping to rest his briny bones.

## Easter Sunday

With teacup between fingertips, I breathe
the smoke from the logging coupes.
When I put down the cup and scratch the back of one hand,
it leaves a chalky mark. I forget to drink enough water. I forget,

too, that I've always had these maps on my hands,
no matter how willfully lost I get in the walking.
Tea tastes like rivers. Perhaps it's
the tannins. Rivers taste like blood. You can see that in the

maps. A snaggled tree out next to the carpark is
holding itself tightly and glowering at
the people facing the coffee machine, backs to the mountain.
Only one side of their faces held in the light.

My children have gone off to their Dad's.
I moved here without him, years ago now,
hoping for a resurrection. The mountain still looks
the same as it did then, but I feel much older. My lips

crackle when I smile back at someone who
thought I was looking at him rather than the mountain
behind his head and shoulders. I'm bothered by the noise
of too many voices. But they don't buffer me from

the quietness of the mountain that keeps
looking at me, and still looks now as I pretend
not to notice and affect that I'm not thinking about it.
Still looking. I avoid its gaze, describe the trees,

memorize faces, miss the kids, and then forget
that my daughter isn't lounging behind me in the armchairs,
long hair falling over her face, and a book, just as mine once did.
The mountain looks. I could never lie to my father. He'd keep

looking and looking until I held his gaze and then there was
no avoiding the truth. He'd follow me down the passageway, leaning
on door jambs all over the house, and if I ran for the yard he'd be
at the back door, while I hid under the lemon tree bending with

the weight of its fruit all the way to the ground. Looking, as I
opened my clenched-shut eyes and peered through the leaves,
grinning when I giggled. Still looking. Relentless,
when I shouted. Nodding, soft-eyed, when I started to cry.

Unyielding, when I tried giggling, shouting and crying at the same
     time.
All ruses exhausted, I'd go quiet, and resist just a little while longer,
inspecting the ground. Still looking. I give in, seeing that the truth is
unchanged but I'm just tired. Twenty-four years ago, he

drowned in a waterway, marked on the maps on the backs of my
     hands,
and still he looks, whenever I avoid the gaze of the truth. Soon I'm
going to walk up the mountain for a gathering. I'll rug up.
It's colder up there, and harder to breathe, closer to the sky.

## Morning, September 4, 2016

So you hope the words you've spoken improved upon the silence
And the songs you've sung improved upon the words
That the acts you've committed brought the songs into your life
And the life you've lived was not for nothing

# CONTRIBUTORS

**Akeema-Zane Anthony** is a multidisciplinary artist of Afro-Caribbean descent who has displayed visual works in various exhibitions, performed in short films/music videos and plays, read her written works and hosted workshops and most recently published liner notes to the album "Conjur Woman." Additionally she has collaborated with various musicians as a featured artist and producer on songs, and is in collaboration for her video directorial debut. Her published works include "There's a Monopoly on Change," "On Being the Daughter Discovering the Home of her Descendants… ," "Interlude," and "When Money Can't Buy You Home." She is a native New Yorker.

**Suhaly Bautista-Carolina,** otherwise known as The Earth Warrior, is an organizer, educator, herbalist, and visual artist. Born in New York City to Afro-Dominican parents, her work is rooted in harnessing and documenting the collective power of community. Before joining the Caribbean Cultural Center African Diaspora Institute (CCCADI) as the director of public programs, Suhaly served as the engagement and education manager at the public art nonprofit, Creative Time. She is the founder of the Afrofuturism book club, Black Magic, and has worked in various capacities with organizations such as The Laundromat Project, Artspace, FOKUS, The Walls-Ortiz Gallery and The Brooklyn Children's Museum. In 2015, she was a panelist at ArtPrize7's "Reflecting the Times: Arts & Activism" alongside Dread Scott and Arts.Black. She is a 2016 alumna of CCCADI's Innovative Cultural Advocacy Fellowship and a graduate of Columbia University's Summer Teachers and Scholars Institute, "The Many Worlds of Black New York." Her photographic documents and writings have been published in *La Galeria Magazine*, United Nations' International Museum of Women and *Caribbean Vistas Journal*. She has enjoyed solo exhibitions at NYU and La Casa Azul Bookstore. As of 2016, Suhaly is a Weeksville Ambassador and serves on the advisory boards to Black Girl Project and More Art. She earned her BA and MPA from NYU, where she was named one of "NYU's 15 Most Influential Students." In 2017, Suhaly joined Brooklyn Museum as a community organizer and is living and loving in Brooklyn with her wife and their daughter, Luna.

**denise h bell** is a mature, published poet. she is a Brooklyn Poets Fellow. The *Village Voice* described her work as "strong, emotional and proud." The *Tinderbox Poetry Journal* nominated her poem, "bitter words," as the 2017 online poem of the year. denise is a proud resident of Brooklyn, NY. she is currently completing her crown sonnet titled: "psalms along myrtle."

**Lawrence William Berggoetz** has been published in *The Bitter Oleander, Sheapshead Review, Pacific Quarterly, Skidrow Penthouse, Stoneboat, Blue Heron Review, Poetry Pacific, JONAH,* and others. He is a graduate of Purdue University and has written the book *Under One Sun.*

**Sylvie Bertrand** is a writer and translator living in Brooklyn. A native French speaker, she was born and grew up in Montreal. She writes poetry, short stories and is working on a novel. Her stories have appeared in several journals, and she was nominated for the 2017 PEN/Robert J. Dau Short Story Prize for Emerging Writers as well as for two Pushcart prizes. One of her stories received a 2018 Pushcart special mention. She teaches memoir and creative writing at The Writers Studio in NYC and is a co-founding editor of *Cagibi,* a literary journal @cagibilit.com. "The Garbage Strike" was a finalist for the Glimmer Train "Very Short Story" contest of July/August 2017.

**Dudgrick Bevins** is a queer interdisciplinary artist who mixes various visual media with poetry. Originally from north Georgia, Dudgrick now resides in New York City with his partner and their very grumpy hedgehog. He teaches literature and creative writing.

**Carl Boon** lives in Izmir, Turkey, where he teaches courses in American culture and literature at 9 Eylül University. His poems appear in dozens of magazines, most recently *The Maine Review* and *The Hawaii Review.* A 2016 Pushcart prize nominee, Boon is currently editing a volume on the sublime in American cultural studies.

**T. Boughnou** was drawn to the writers and thinkers of the nineteenth and early twentieth centuries. After years of a dedicated reading and writing regimen and journal-keeping of his thoughts and observations of his daily routines and personal travels, he began to write. He lives in the greater Boston area, where he works as a wellness specialist.

**Kim Darlene Brandon** advanced her studies in fiction writing at the New School and by attending the North Country Institute for Writers of Color Retreats at Medgar Evers College, Brooklyn Society Writer's Group, Women of Color Writers, Hurston/Wright Workshop, and New York Writers' Coalition. She is published in the anthology *The Dream Catcher's Song.*

**Bridget Bufford** leads creative writing workshops using the Amherst Writers & Artists method. She's the editor of *Eternal as a Weed: Tales of Ozark Experience from Creative Writing of Columbia,* and author of *Cemetery Bird* and *Minus One: A Twelve-Step Journey.* Shorter works have appeared in fat anthologies and thin litmags.

**Marissa Cagan** lives in western Massachusetts with her high school sweetheart. She hopes to write a novel someday.

**Marian Calabro** writes poems, prose, and plays. She lives in New Jersey and has been an AWA workshop leader since 2004.

**Christopher Cascio** took his MFA at Stony Brook University's Southampton Arts, where he studied with Susan Scarf Merrell, Lou Ann Walker, Roger Rosenblatt, and Zachary Lazar. His writing has appeared in *The Southampton Review*, *The Feathertale Review*, *Kalliope*, and *Rose & Thorn Journal*. He teaches writing at Monroe College and also works as a freelance editor and visual artist. He currently lives in Kings Park, NY, with his dog, Samuel L. Jackson III.

**Megan Colleen Choate** received her BA in English from Cal Poly San Luis Obispo. Her senior thesis, "The Poet's Ampersand," is an exploration and collection of her poetry written in college. Since graduating, she has continued on to graduate school for teaching, wishing to build compassion and empathy in the next generation through literature. She hopes in some capacity her writing resonates with readers, bringing a connection through the ethereal essence that is art.

**Bethany Clem** lives in a small town in Texas with her four children. She lives by the motto, "Don't make your skeletons stay in the closet." They are your testimony and keep you humble. Never know when they may be used to help someone else. She spends her days caring for her children, writing, quilting, and shopping at flea markets.

**Janel Cloyd** is a poet, essayist, and fiction writer. She has been awarded fellowships with The Watering Hole and Willow Artist Alliance/Willow Books. Her work appears in *The Anthologies: Black Lives Have Always Mattered*, *The Mujeres*, *The Magic*, *The Muse*. She is also included in Poeming Pigeon and Yellow Chair publications.

**Jona Colson's** poems have been published in *The Southern Review*, *Beloit Poetry Journal*, *Subtropics*, *Prairie Schooner*, *The Massachusetts Review*, and elsewhere. Her first collection of poetry recently won the Jean Feldman Poetry Prize from the Washington Writers' Publishing House.

**Tricia Coscia** is an MFA student in Bluegrass Writers Studio Low-Residency Program and works for Witness to Innocence, a program that supports and empowers death-row exonerees in their advocacy to end the death penalty. A runner-up for 2017 Bucks County, PA, Poet Laureate, her poems have appeared in *A&U: America's AIDS Magazine*, the anthology *Literature from the First Twenty Years of A&U*, *Many Colored Brooms*, *Parting Gifts*, and will soon be featured in the 2018 anthology, *50/50: Poems & Translations by Women Over 50* (Quills Edge Press), and *Connecticut River Review*. Tricia lives in Morrisville, PA, with her husband Joe, their children and a menagerie.

**Anne Dellenbaugh** is a wilderness guide, ayurvedic practitioner, yoga and meditation instructor. Anne knows, first-hand, both the great joys and the full catastrophe of life in a body. A transplanted Mainer, she currently lives in Santa Fe, NM.

**Tania De Rozario** is an artist and writer based in Singapore. She is the author of *And The Walls Come Crumbling Down* (2016, Math Paper Press) and *Tender Delirium* (2013, Math Paper Press). Her work won the 2011 Singapore Golden Point Award for Poetry, was shortlisted for the 2014 Singapore Literature Prize, and has been showcased in Asia, USA, UK, and Europe. She is a two-time recipient of Singapore's National Arts Council's Creation Grant, and she runs EtiquetteSG, a platform that develops and showcases art, writing, and film by women. Her written work can be found in various literary spaces, including the *Santa Fe Writers Project, Softblow Poetry Journal, Blue Lyra Review, Sow's Ear Poetry Review, Prairie Schooner Online Journal,* and *Burningword Literary Journal.*

**Tarianne DeYonker** lives in Adrian, MI, and is a member of the Dominican Sisters of Adrian. She has taught elementary and junior high school, been a family therapist, a community organizer, held numerous leadership positions and has traveled worldwide. As a new graduate of AWA training, she is beginning to lead writing groups in her local area.

**Joël Díaz** is a writer and educator based in New York City. His work has been featured in *The Feminist Wire, Interviewing the Caribbean,* and *Africana Heritage.* He is Watering Hole Fellow and a 2017 Callaloo Fellow.

**Ken Allan Dronsfield** is a poet who was nominated for The Best of the Net and two Pushcart Awards for Poetry in 2016. His poetry has been published worldwide in various publications throughout North and South America, Europe, Asia, Australia and Africa. His work has appeared in *The Burningword Journal, Belle Reve Journal, Setu Magazine, The Literary Hatchet Magazine, The Stray Branch, Now/Then Manchester Magazine, Bewildering Stories, Scarlet Leaf Review, EMBOSS Magazine* and many more. Ken loves thunderstorms, walking in the woods at night, and spending time with his cat Willa. His new book, *The Cellaring,* a collection of haunting, paranormal, weird and wonderful poems, has been released and is available through Amazon.com. He is the co-editor of two poetry anthologies, *Moonlight Dreamers of Yellow Haze* and *Dandelion in a Vase of Roses,* available from Amazon.com.

**Annie Fahy,** nationally known trainer in the areas of motivational interviewing, harm reduction, reducing compassion-fatigue, and working with difficult patients, is an RN and an LCSW. She specializes in difficult populations. Her writing credits include two chapters in *The Praeger Handbook of Community Health* on "Addictions and Aging" and "Substance Use Disorders" (2014, 2017). She also published an article called "The Unbearable Fatigue of Compassion: Notes from a Substance

Abuse Counselor Who Dreams of Working at Starbuck's" (2007, *The Journal of Social Work*). Her poem "Yoko" was a winner in the fifth annual Pat Schneider Writing Contest published in Peregrine, 2016. Her first book of poetry, *The Glass Train*, was published by Amherst Writers & Artists Press in 2017. She often publishes poetry and essays on the social platform: medium at https://medium.com/@AnnieOFahy.

**Lisa Favicchia** is a recent graduate of the MFA program at Bowling Green State University and the former managing editor of *Mid-American Review*. Her work has appeared in *Smeuse Poetry, Vine Leaves Literary Journal*, and Wordpool Press, among others, and is forthcoming in *Rubbertop Review, The Airgonaut*, and *Adelaide Literary Magazine*.

**Leigh Fisher** is from New Jersey and works in an office by day, but she is a writer around the clock. She is a historical fiction enthusiast, with an avid interest in Chinese history. She has been published in *Five 2 One Magazine, The Missing Slate, Heater Magazine*, and *Referential Magazine*.

**Fletch Fletcher** is a science teacher, a poet, a brother, a friend, and an observer of how all people connect to everything around them. We need to strive for connection if we are to ever be better than we are.

**Lauren Foley** is Irish and Australian (enough). Her short stories are published internationally. In 2016, Lauren won the inaugural Neilma Sidney Award with *Overland Literary Journal*, was highly commended for the Over the Edge New Writer of the Year Award, and shortlisted for the @ Writing.ie#BGEIBAS Short Story of the Year. She was further awarded a 2016 Varuna Residential Writer's Fellowship and shortlisted for the Irish Times Hennessy Literary Awards, 2017. Lauren has systemic lupus erythematosus (SLE), and lives in Skerries, County Dublin. laurenfoleywriter.com @AYearinSouthOz.

**Moya Hegarty** is an Ursuline Sister. Brought up in an Irish-speaking home, she has worked in retreat ministry in Ireland, UK, Israel, Kenya, and Pakistan. She has published two books for children, *The Button Bath* and *The Rainbow Button*. She writes commentaries on both Jewish and Christian scriptures.

**Brad Johnson's** full-length poetry collection, *The Happiness Theory* (Main Street, 2013) is available at mainstreetrag.com/bookstore/product-tag/brad-johnson/. Work of his has also been accepted by *Hayden's Ferry Review, J Journal, New Madrid, Meridian, Poet Lore, Salamander, Southern Indiana Review, Tampa Review, Tar River Poetry*, and others.

**Jacqueline Johnson** is a multi-disciplined artist creating in both poetry and fiction writing. She is the author of *A Woman's Season*, Main Street Rag Press, and *A Gathering of Mother Tongues*, White Pine Press, and is the winner of the third annual White Pine Press Poetry Award. Recent publications include *The Brooklyn Poets Anthology, Revise the Psalm:*

*Work Celebrating the Writing of Gwendolyn Brooks,* and *Speculating Futures: Black Imagination and the Arts.* Works in progress include *The Privilege of Memory* and *Songs of Ikari,* a collection of short stories. A native of Philadelphia, she resides in Brooklyn.

**Kenneth Kapp** was a research mathematician, starving artist, systems engineer, and dot com geek. He still continues home brewing and teaching yoga. His day job, in the early morning hours, is writing.

**Gretchen Krull** is program director for Voices From Inside, an organization that provides writing workshops for incarcerated and previously incarcerated women and women in recovery. Her inspiration comes from these writers and countless women she has worked with over her career. Empowering women to speak out proudly is her passion.

**Kelly E. Largent** is a physician and writer in Asheville, NC. She practices internal medicine, enjoys roaming the beautiful western North Carolina outdoors and writes at her favorite coffee shops.

**Anne Lorda,** empty-nested at seventy-seven years of age, on a dirt road in Cummington, MA, still lives in wonderment.... And she can now recite "The Windhover" flawlessly.

**Beth MacFarlane**, a jack of all trades, master of some, finds happiness in making things. Now in her fifth decade, she has turned her creative energy towards words. Her work has appeared in *Abridged, Torrid Literature Journal,* and *Poeming Pigeons.* Beth lives in Montclair, NJ.

**Ariel S. Maloney** teaches literature and writing to high school students in Cambridge, MA. She earned a BA in English at the University of New Hampshire, where she studied poetry under Mekeel McBride, and an MEd at Harvard. Her poetry and nonfiction have appeared in publications such as *The Inman Review, Around the World: An Anthology of Travel Writing, The Huffington Post, The Ekphrastic Review, Commonwealth Magazine, The Jewish Advocate,* and more.

**Diane T. Masucci** is working in historical fiction. A former journalist, she writes essays and short stories and lives in Montclair, NJ.

**Bernadette D. McComish** went to Hunter College to study creative writing with Colum McCann, Donna Masini, and Elena Georgiou. After completing her BA, she knew writing was her passion, poetry was her lifeline, and teaching paid the bills. In 2009 she earned an MFA in poetry at Sarah Lawrence College where she worked with Marie Howe, Dennis Nurkse, Kate Knapp Johnson, and Joy Ladin. In May 2014, she completed a second master's degree in teaching English as a second language. Currently she teaches high school in LA, performs with the Poetry Brothel, Melrose Poetry Bureau, and the Poetry Society of New York. Her chapbook, *The Book of Johns,* is forthcoming in 2018 from

Dancing Girl Press. She won first prize for faculty writing while she was an adjunct at CUNY's New York City College of Technology, and her poems have been published in *The Cortland Review, Sunday Salon, Hakol, Hospital Drive, Slipstream, Storyscape, Rag Queen Periodical, Flapper House,* and *deluge,* and she was a finalist for the New Millennium Writers 41st Poetry Prize.

**Robert John Miller's** work has appeared in *dogzplot, Bartleby Snopes* and *Monkeybicycle.* He is an Amherst Writers & Artists affiliate, certified to lead workshops in the AWA method.

**Kyle Mola** is a poet from Stonington, CT. He recently returned from a year in Wales, where he received his MA in creative writing/poetry.

**Matthew Olson-Roy** is a graduate student in creative writing at the University of Oxford. He is a Pushcart Prize-nominated author and 2018 SCBWI Undiscovered Voices winner. His children's book, *Humonstromous,* was recently published in *Bedtime Stories—Read & Tell.* He lives in Luxembourg with his husband and their two children.

**Elaine Olund** writes and works in Cincinnati, Ohio, when not wandering around laughing and crying in random places. She writes poems, stories, novels and things that are hard to label. Walk, stretch, read, write, repeat. Find her at elaineolund.com.

**Richard King Perkins II** is a state-sponsored advocate for residents in long-term care facilities. He lives in Crystal Lake, IL, with his wife, Vickie, and daughter, Sage. He is a three-time Pushcart Prize, Best of the Net and Best of the Web nominee whose work has appeared in more than a thousand publications.

**Indigo Perry's** book *Midnight Water: A Memoir* (Picador) was shortlisted for Australia's National Biography Award. She teaches creative writing at Deakin University, Melbourne, Australia. Most of Indigo's current writing is poetry, often written live in performance as part of the improvisational performance art duo Illuminous.

**David Pontrelli** lives in Hartford, CT, and is a certified Amherst Writers & Artists workshop leader for underserved populations. He likes leading writing groups for working people, and the children of working people, and holds workshops at public libraries, community centers, for GED programs, churches, and other non-profit organizations.

**Audra Puchalski** lives and weaves small tapestries in Oakland, CA.

**Gopal Raman**, a student at Stanford University, was chosen for the 2016 Class of National Student Poets, the nation's highest award for youth poets, by the President's Committee on the Arts and Humanities and select other jurors. He is studying computer science, philosophy, and poetry in addition to playing tennis and tutoring. He has held readings and spoken at the White House, Smithsonian American Art Museum, Dodge Poetry Festival, Aspen Ideas Festival, and TEDxPlano.

**Brett Ramseyer** teaches English and creative publishing in Hart, MI, where he and his wife raise their three children. He earned a 2013 Norman Mailer Semifinalist for Teachers of English in creative non-fiction. He published his first novel, *Come Not to Us,* in 2014 and a collection of short fiction, *Waiting For Bells,* in 2016.

**Grace Redman** is from the San Francisco Bay area and is currently attending NYU for a BFA in interactive media arts. She is the eleventh-grade winner of the Maeve Poetry Award, a successful Nanowrimo participant and a Power of the Pen trophy winner. In her spare time she enjoys trying new foods and complaining about New York winters.

**Susan Lynn Reynolds** is a writer, teacher, and psychotherapist. Her specialty is writing for therapeutic benefit. She teaches writing through workshops in the community, in college continuing education programs, and in social services settings. She has been leading writing workshops for female inmates at Central East Correctional Centre on a volunteer basis for twelve years. She writes and has won awards for her YA novel, short stories, poems, and non-fiction.

**Christina Ruest** is my name. I am data and program coordinator at Friends of the Homeless, which is a program of Clinical & Support Options. I am also a board member and treasurer for Voices From Inside. I myself am a previously incarcerated woman who has struggled with heroin addiction. I have now been in recovery for nine years, and I have successfully finished my bachelor's degree. I would not be where I am today without writing. I am a testament to how creativity and writing can heal.

**Margaret Sáraco's** poetry has appeared in *Shalom: The Jewish Peace Newsletter, Free Verse Literary Magazine, Poet's Online,* anthologies *Just Bite Me, Passing* and *Italians and the Arts.* Featured readings include "Welcome the Sabbath Bride with Poetry and Song," "Poetry U: An Evening of Spoken Word," "The Art and Poetry of Teaching," which she also co-produced, and the JCC MetroWest Poetry Series. Margaret lives in Montclair, NJ, where she teaches middle-school mathematics and is the local teacher's union treasurer.

**Constance Schultz** lives in the Pacific northwest with her daughter and Winston the dog. She has had a poem published in the *Calamus Journal* and more are forthcoming in *Stonecoast Review Literary Magazine, Figroot Press, sea foam mag* and *Blue Noon Lit Mag.*

**Alexandra Smith** writes in a cabin in the woods of Massachusetts, with a house full of dogs and cats.

**Elizabeth Upshur**, a graduate student at Western Kentucky University Bowling Green, is studying creative writing with a secondary concentration in literature. She is a member of Sigma Delta Pi National Collegiate Hispanic Honor Society, Phi Theta Kappa, and was a Who's Who Among Students in American Universities and Colleges recipient. She has participated in Meacham Writers Workshop, Frost Place Conference on Poetry, and Bread Loaf Translators' Conference. Her work has been published in several student and regional journals, including Perceptions, Red Mud Review, Zephyrus, and Lost River. She has presented papers and/or research at several local conferences, including the first Tennessee Experiential Learning Symposium and is excited to be presenting at the Robert Penn Warren Circle. Her current research interests include Mark Twain, translation, feminine monsters, and Black spirituality. In her free time, she enjoys listening to music, sketching, and bachata dancing.

**Lee V.** is my name. I was born in 1990 and use my art to show what's inside. Thank you for having an open heart and fair mind.

**Pam Van Dyk** holds an MFA in creative writing from Queens University of Charlotte. She is a member of the NC Writers' Network, Women's Fiction Writers Association, and Sisters in Crime. Her work has been anthologized in *Juxtaposition* (Maine Review, 2015), *Home* (Outrider Press, 2016), and *Flying South* (Winston-Salem Writers, 2016). She has been a Top 25 (2014) and honorable mention Glimmer Train recipient (2016), and her stories have been awarded honors by The Writers' Workshop of Asheville (literary fiction contest) and Women on Writing (flash fiction contest). Her online journal publications include works at *Fiction on the Web, Crack the Spine,* and *Mamalode.*

**Susan Whelehan** facilitates AWA workshops in her home in Toronto, Canada, as well as in her local seniors' center. This work makes her very happy. Her poetry has won first place in the Canadian Church Press Awards, has been short-listed in the CBC Canada Writes Competition, and has been included in several Canadian journals, anthologies, newspapers and once in *Peregrine*. If you are reading this, it is because her work is again in *Peregrine*!

**Mimi Whittaker** has been writing since early childhood and lives in Northern California. She has one son and two grandchildren and still enjoys time with her ninety-year-old mother. Raised in upstate New York, she often finds her writing travels back to the Hudson River and the Adirondack Mountains as often as it does the beautiful coast of California. What informs her work most are the people who have shaped her life. She may stop writing and teaching someday, but probably not until some other fat lady sings.

**Holly Wiegand** is a graduate student at Boston University, studying English. A Montana native, she enjoys fly fishing, kayaking, skiing, and discovering what it means to be human. Her work has previously appeared in *DASH Literary Journal* and *Polaris Literary Magazine*.

**Mary Zaliznock** writes poetry and fiction. She is currently working on a novel exploring the complexities of love, loss, and forgiveness. She is happiest doing active things in warm and sunny places. This is her first publication.

# *Peregrine*
## THE JOURNAL OF AMHERST WRITERS & ARTISTS

*Peregrine* has provided a forum for national and international writers since 1983, and is committed to finding exceptional work by both emerging and established writers. We seek work that is unpretentious, memorable, and reflects diversity of voice. We accept only original and unpublished poetry and short stories. No work for or by children. *Peregrine*, published by Amherst Writers & Artists Press, is staffed by volunteers. All decisions are made by the editors after all submissions have arrived, so our response time may be slower than that of other literary journals. We welcome simultaneous submissions.

**Poetry**: Three to five single-spaced, one-page poems. We seek poems that inform and surprise us.

**Prose**: Short stories, double-spaced, 3,000 words maximum (include word count on first page); shorter stories have a better chance.

For additional submission details, please see www.amherstwriters. com or peregrinejournal.submittable.com. All submissions are via submittable.com unless other arrangements are made.

Additional copies of this issue are available at Amazon.com for $12.

**The Editors**
Amherst Writers & Artists Press
P.O. Box 1076
Amherst, MA 01004
www.amherstwriters.org

Made in the USA
Monee, IL
13 October 2022